BRADFORD STREET BUDDIES
Block Party Surprise

For Cyndie, the planner —J.N.

For Chris, Eden, and Briar, forever and for always —M.H.

Text copyright © 2015 by Jerdine Nolen
Illustrations copyright © 2015 by Michelle Henninger

For information about permission to reproduce selections from this book,
write to Permissions, Houghton Mifflin Harcourt Publishing Company, 215
Park Avenue South, New York, New York 10003.

www.hmhco.com

The text of this book is set in Chaparral Pro.
The display type was set in Candy Round and Marujo.
The illustrations are drawn ink and watercolor on Arches watercolor paper.

Library of Congress Cataloging-in-Publication Data
Nolen, Jerdine.
Block party surprise / by Jerdine Nolen.
p. cm. — (The Bradford Street buddies ; book 1) (Green light readers. Level 3)
Summary: Mr. Perkins has a big surprise for the annual block party, but when
the truck carrying it there breaks down, twins Jada and Jamal and their best
friends, Josh and Carlita, propose a different form of transportation.
ISBN 978-0-544-35863-8 paperback
ISBN 978-0-544-35862-1 paper over board
[1. Parties—Fiction. 2. Robots—Fiction. 3. Friendship—Fiction. 4. Brothers and
sisters—Fiction. 5. Twins—Fiction. 6. African Americans—Fiction.] I. Title.
PZ7.N723Bjs 2015
[E]—dc23
2014006758

Manufactured in China
SCP 10 9 8 7 6 5 4 3 2 1
4500530036

BRADFORD STREET BUDDIES
Block Party Surprise

WRITTEN BY **JERDINE NOLEN**

ILLUSTRATED BY **MICHELLE HENNINGER**

Green Light Readers
HOUGHTON MIFFLIN HARCOURT
Boston New York

CONTENTS

1. The Big Day   1

2. Backyard Stomp   11

3. Let's Get Ready!   21

4. A Big Problem   29

1. The Big Day

Jada Perkins was excited. She jumped out of bed. Today was the Bradford Street Fall Block Party. It was going to be a day full of friends, fun, and surprises.

"Wake up, Jamal," Jada shouted as she passed by her twin brother's bedroom. "Carlita should be here any minute. She wants to see the big surprise Dad is bringing to the block party."

"That's right! Today's the block party,"
remembered Jamal. Muzzy barked and pounced on
him. "Josh is meeting me here too," he called back to
his sister. "I wonder what the big surprise will be."
"I do too!" replied Jada. "I can't believe Dad kept it a
secret this long."

THUMP, THUMP, BUMP, BUMP!
Jada and Jamal heard a noise.
It thumped and bumped past the window.
There it was again.
THUMP, THUMP, BUMP, BUMP!

"What was that?" asked Jada.

"Only one way to find out," answered Jamal, hopping out of bed.

They raced to the window.

They could not believe what they saw.

"Dinosaurs!" they shrieked.

"ONE . . . TWO . . . THREE . . . FOUR."

They counted four robotic dinosaurs in their backyard!

Mr. Perkins was tinkering with the Triceratops.

Josh's dad, Mr. Cornell, was painting the tail of

the Tyrannosaurus rex.

Mrs. Perkins was working the controls
of the Brachiosaurus.

Mrs. Garcia, Carlita's mom, was taking pictures of
the Stegosaurus.

"Hi, Dad! Hi, Mom!" Jamal called.

"What's going on down there?" asked Jada.

"Get dressed and come and see," Mrs. Perkins shouted.

Mr. Cornell waved and said, "We parents can't have all the fun!"

"That's right," laughed Mrs. Garcia.

Jada and Jamal got dressed in a hurry.

They zoomed out the door.

Muzzy followed right along.

2. Backyard Stomp

"There's Josh and Carlita." Jamal pointed and waved
to their best friends.

"Hurry," Jada called. "You've got to see this!"

"Dinosaurs?" Carlita giggled as she entered the backyard. "Wow! They look amazing."

"I'm glad they aren't as big as real ones," laughed Josh. "We'd never be able to handle them!"

"Dad, can we work the controls?" Jada asked.

"Could we? Could we?" pleaded Jamal.

"That's what I had in mind," Mr. Perkins said.

"Look!" Carlita pointed. "Muzzy likes the Triceratops, too."

"I like the T. rex," Josh said.

"I want the Brachiosaurus," Jamal said.

"The Stegosaurus is my favorite," Jada squealed.

Carlita announced, "The Triceratops can walk in circles."

"Look," Jamal said. "I can make the Brachiosaurus touch a leaf."

"My Tyrannosaurus rex can roar," said Josh.

"My Stegosaurus can bang its tail," Jada laughed.

17

TWEEEEET! Mrs. Perkins blew her handy whistle. "It's time to put the dinosaurs away. We have to get ready for the party," she said.

"We'll bring the dinosaurs to the party when the truck arrives," explained Mr. Perkins.

"Can we ride on the truck with the dinosaurs?" Jamal asked.

"Yes," Mr. Perkins said. "We also need your help to demonstrate how they work."

"I want everyone to see them," Jada said, hugging her dad. "Dinosaurs are the best surprise you've ever brought home!"

3. Let's Get Ready!

Mr. Cornell was ready to paint the Welcome banner.

"Want some help?" Josh asked.

"Sure," Mr. Cornell answered.

"Jamal and I are best at drawing dinosaurs," said Josh.
"Do you think we should add pictures of the dinosaurs
to the banner, too?"

"Absolutely!" Mr. Cornell said.

The kids started painting right away.

Bradford
Street
Park

The sign looked nice.

It read:

Welcome to the Bradford Street Fall Block Party! Let's have BIG fun!

"When the banner dries, I will need help hanging it up," said Mr. Cornell. "In the meantime, we can set up some chairs."

"Maybe I should see if my mom needs help setting up the food," Carlita said.

"I'll come too," Jada agreed.

"I'll race you to the picnic tables," Carlita giggled.

Carlita's mother and grandmother were arranging the dessert table.

"We're here to help," Carlita said.

"Thanks," said Mrs. Garcia. "You can start by putting out the plates and napkins. Then you can help with the cupcake display."

"Look," Jada said, licking her lips. "Your mom decorated the cupcakes with dinosaurs!"

"Now the cupcakes are delicious and cute," Carlita said.

In a little while Jamal and Josh came by.

"We had to put up the banner without you," Josh said.

"How does it look?" asked Jada.

"It's perfect," said Jamal.

TWEEEEET! TWEEEEET! That was the sound of
Mrs. Perkins's whistle.

The kids went running.

Hooray! It was time to bring the dinosaurs to the
block party!

4. A Big Problem

"Kids, we have a problem," Mrs. Perkins said.

"The truck broke down," Mr. Perkins explained.

"Can it be fixed?" Jamal asked.

"Not on such short notice," Mr. Perkins said.

"Is there another truck we can borrow?" asked Jada.

"Not in time for the party," Mrs. Perkins said.

"What about our van?" Josh asked.

"Good idea, but it's not big enough," Mr. Cornell said.

"What are we going to do about the dinosaurs?"
 Jamal asked.

"We might not be able to bring them to the party,"
 Mr. Perkins said.

"Oh no!" cried Jada.

"What if we could find another way to get the
dinosaurs to the party?" Jamal asked.

"Hmmmm," Mr. Perkins said, rubbing his chin.

"We can at least try," Carlita said.

"Yes," agreed Mrs. Perkins.

"As I always say, go to it!"

TWEEEEET! TWEEEEET!

The kids formed a huddle.

"The problem is," Jada began, "we need something with wheels and space to carry the dinosaurs."

"We have a cart with wheels," Carlita said. "I use it to help deliver pastries for my mom's deli."

"We have a wheelbarrow," Jada said. "I use it to help with the gardening."

"And I have a wagon," Jamal said.

"We could load the dinosaurs and wheel them to the party," Jamal said.

"It would be just like a parade," Jada said. "It could be the first Bradford Street Dinosaur Parade!"

Everyone cheered.

"Well, kids," Mrs. Perkins said, "go to it!"
TWEEET!

"But what about you, Josh?" Jamal asked.

"Do you have anything with wheels?"

"I think I have a great idea!" said Josh.

"I'll be right back."

Josh went running toward his house.

Mr. and Mrs. Perkins helped the kids load the dinosaurs.
Mr. Cornell helped tie them down.

They loaded the Triceratops onto the cart.
The Brachiosaurus went on the wagon.
The Stegosaurus fit on the wheelbarrow.

It was getting late.
"Where's Josh?" Jamal wondered.

"Here I am," Josh yelled. "I think the T. rex should skateboard to the party!"
Everyone cheered.

"This is going to be the best block party ever," Jada announced.

And it was!